NEW BOY IN SCHOOL

by May Justus

Cover design by Elle Staples

Cover illustration by Joan Balfour Payne

and Ecaterina Leascenco

Inside illustrations by Joan Balfour Payne

First published in 1963

Table of Contents

I wish I was an ap-ple, an ap-ple on a tree, I'd

hang so high no-bod-y could climb up af-ter me.

1

Lennie Lane's family moved from Newton, Louisiana, to Nashville, Tennessee, in the middle of the school year. The day that they arrived in their new home was Lennie's birthday. He was seven years old.

He wasn't very happy on this birthday. In the hurry and scurry of moving, there had been no time for a birthday party like the one he had last year. His mother had even been too busy to bake a cake for Lennie. All he had to be happy about was a pair of new shoes that he hadn't been allowed to wear yet.

Lennie didn't like the idea of going to school among strangers. He wished his folks had stayed on in Newton where he knew all the boys and girls in first grade and Miss Ellen, the teacher.

His father explained over and over why it was best to move.

"In Nashville, we'll have a nicer house in a good neighborhood," he told Lennie. "I'll have a better job with more pay. You'll have a better school. The boss has promised me all this. It's a step up for me—a big one. That's why we are moving."

Lennie's father belonged to a crew of workmen who built houses for a large construction company. He went from place to place with them. They worked on one job, finished it, and then went on to another.

The Lanes had never lived more than a year in any town or city. They didn't mind this, but

they always hoped that their next home would
be better than the last.

As Lennie's father talked about the reasons
for moving, Lennie was ashamed to grumble,
even though he felt grumbly inside. He
thought about his birthday shoes, shiny brown
with golden stitching. He would wear them
tomorrow when he started at the new school.
This made Lennie feel a little more cheerful,

even though he didn't want to face all those
strange children.

Lennie was glad to have new shoes on that
first morning when his father and mother took

him to Miss Baker's room. It wasn't a bit like
his old school. It had been an unpainted house
which had only one room and one teacher for
the whole school. The walls had many cracks
and only a few windows. Miss Baker's room
had clean, bright walls, with colorful pictures,
and so many windows that it seemed almost
like having school outdoors. In the back of the

room, there was a play corner full of toys, a shelf of picture books, a bird in a yellow cage, and a fish bowl.

"A wonderful school," Lennie's mother said as Miss Baker showed them about the new place.

"A good school," Lennie's father said. "I am glad our boy can come here."

Lennie said nothing. Somehow he was a little afraid in this fine new school. It all seemed so strange to him. Most of the faces about him were friendly—Miss Baker's and those of the children—but they were white faces.

"There are so many of them," said Lennie, "and only one of me." Yes, Lennie was the only black boy in the room.

"This," Lennie's father explained, "is an integrated school."

"What does integrated mean?" Lennie asked.

"That means it is a school where black children and white children study and play together," the father explained.

"Yes," said the teacher. "There are other black children in the school, but you are the only one in this room."

Lennie felt too shy to say what he was thinking. He was wishing that at least half the children in that room had brown faces instead of white.

"You'll feel more at home with us later," Miss Baker said, smiling down at him as if she understood.

When his father and mother told him goodbye and started to leave him, Lennie clung to them and nearly burst into tears.

"Be a good boy," his father whispered. His mother said nothing, but she gave him a quick hug.

Then his parents were gone. Lennie heard a door close. He heard the voice of the teacher say: "Come, sit here by Terry. He is making something out of clay he might like to show you."

Lennie sat down, but he wouldn't even look at Terry or what he was doing. He still

wanted to cry. So he picked up a big book that
was lying nearby and hid behind it for a long
time. Sometimes he peeped around the book
at the other children. Once he saw two boys
whispering as they looked at him.

"They are talking about me," Lennie thought.

One of the boys was smiling.

"He is laughing at me," Lennie said to
himself. "I am the only black boy here. That's
why they are laughing."

This thought made Lennie very sad. He
wished he were not in this school with so many
white faces all around him. He wished he was
back in the old tumble-down school where
all the children were friendly. Here he had no
friends at all.

Lennie thought of slipping out the door and
running home to his mother. He would tell
her how he hated this new school. He would
beg her to let him stay at home. Perhaps he
could talk his father into moving back to
the old home.

Just then he felt a hand on his shoulder.
Lennie looked up. It was Terry, with a grin
on his face.

"Come over here," he said. "I'll show you
what I've been making—a little horse."

But Lennie felt too shy to follow Terry. He
only shook his head and settled farther down in
his chair behind the big book.

When it was time for reading class, Lennie
paid no attention. He just sat there behind
his book. When it was time for recess, and all
the children ran outside, Lennie stayed in the
schoolroom.

Finally, Miss Baker took him by the hand and
tried to get him to join in a singing game. As
soon as she turned him loose, though, Lennie
ran off. When the children laughed at him, he

hid behind a big bush that grew in a corner of the schoolyard.

It wasn't a happy day for Lennie. When it was over, he was glad to find his father and mother waiting to take him home.

"How was school today?" his father asked as they started off.

Lennie drew a deep breath. He might as well get it over. "I don't like that school, and I don't want to go back tomorrow."

"Oh, you'd better try it another day, at least once more," said his father. "You may like it better by this time tomorrow. I'd try it another day if I were you."

"That's a good idea," said his mother. "Your father is a smart man. You had better do what he says."

Lennie's father nodded.

"One reason we moved here," he said, "was so that you could go to such a fine school. It's one of the very best in the city—the first to be integrated."

"In-te-grated." Lennie said the word slowly. He remembered that word and his father's explanation: "An integrated school is a place where black children and white children study and play together."

Lennie shook his head. "They don't like me because I'm a black. And I don't like them," he added, "because they don't like me." He sounded all mixed up, but this was the way he felt inside.

"When they get used to you, they'll be friendly," said his father. "But you must be friendly, too. That's how to make friends—on a job—or going to school."

Lennie remembered Terry, who had wanted to show him his horse. Terry had tried to be friendly. He had looked surprised when Lennie wouldn't go with him to see his work.

As Lennie remembered Terry, he thought of what he might do tomorrow. "I guess I could stand that new school for just one more day," he said.

2

Lennie was early at school the next day.
Miss Baker seemed glad to see him. She took
him over to the worktable and gave him a big
lump of clay.

"See what you can make out of this," she said.

All around the big table were things that the
other children had made. Lennie saw a horse
and guessed that this might belong to Terry. It
was a fine little horse. It looked almost alive, as
if it were ready to run. "It is good, but it ought
to have a rider," thought Lennie.

All at once he had an idea. Quickly he began to work with the clay. He was so busy that he paid no attention to what was going on around him. Soon he had made a little man.

"That looks like a cowboy." It was Terry who had come up behind him.

Lennie nodded. "I made him for you. He is to ride on your horse," he said. Terry took the cowboy and set him in place.

"Yes, they look fine together, don't they? Thank you, Lennie," Terry said with a smile.

"You're welcome," Lennie answered, smiling back.

That day when Lennie got home from school, his father and mother were waiting to ask him, "How did you get along in school today?"

"I got along okay," Lennie replied. "I like school a little better on account of Terry." And he went on to explain. "Terry and I are friends. We do things together." He told them about what Terry and he had made.

Lennie's mother smiled happily. "I am glad to hear this."

Lennie's father nodded. "I am glad, too," he said. "Now you have found one friend. Soon you will have others. Just remember what I told you. Act in a friendly way to all your schoolmates. This is the way to make them like you."

Lennie thought of Jack and Joe, the two boys who had laughed at him. He didn't feel friendly toward them. He didn't like them at all, and he didn't think they would ever be his friends.

Lennie started to tell his thoughts, but he stopped because his father had just pulled something from his pocket. It was a round package tied with string.

"Here's something you might like to take to school tomorrow," he said with a smile.

Lennie's eager fingers fumbled with the string. Even before it was untied, he had guessed what was in the package.

A moment later, he was bouncing it up and down on the floor. It was a beautiful red-white-and-blue ball.

"Thank you, Daddy!" cried Lennie. "This is the prettiest ball I ever saw. Tomorrow I'll take it to school and show it to Terry. I'll let him play with it, too, because he is my friend."

The next day at morning recess, Lennie and Terry went off to a corner of the playground to play all by themselves.

"Let's play bounce ball," Terry said. "This ball is made of rubber and is just the right kind."

Lennie had never played bounce ball, but he listened while Terry explained.

"When I bounce the ball on the ground, you must try to catch it," Terry said. "You have to catch it on the bounce—not when it's rolling. When you miss, it's my turn."

Lennie thought this was a very fine game.

While he and Terry were playing, some of the other children came over to watch them. Among them were Jack and Joe, but Lennie paid no attention to them. He kept on playing with Terry.

"What a dandy ball!" he heard Jack say.

"It's better than the one we lost," said Joe.

"I wonder if we could join this game," Jack said to Joe.

Lennie looked up quickly to see if these boys were joking, but they weren't laughing at him. They weren't making fun of him.

"Do you think they really want to play with us?" Lennie asked Terry in a low tone. "Is it all right to let them into the game?"

"I think it would be more fun," Terry said, "to have more boys playing. That is, if you are willing," he added. "It's your ball."

Lennie bounced the ball toward Jack and Joe.

"Catch, *anybody*!" he cried.

Jack and Joe ran forward and bumped into each other. Jack fell down, and it was Joe who got hold of the ball.

"Whoop-ee!" he yelled, but he was so excited that he dropped the ball before he could bounce it even once.

Now Lennie had it again.

"Here! Here!" someone shouted. He looked up and saw that the nearest boy was Joe.

"Here!" he answered, and threw it to him.

Just then Miss Baker came out to watch the game. She had an idea.

"Why not have two teams and play for the highest score?" she suggested.

All of the boys thought this a fine plan. They elected Lennie and Terry for captains. Miss

Baker kept score. Sometimes Lennie's side was ahead. Sometimes it was Terry's. At the end of playtime, there was a tie.

"We'll break the tie later," said Miss Baker, "at the next play period."

As they started back to the schoolroom, Lennie put the ball in his pocket and went with Terry and Jack and Joe to the front of the line.

That night when Lennie got home, his folks asked the usual questions:

"Do you like school any better?"

"How did you get along today?"

Lennie was ready to answer: "I like school a little better. We had a big ball game today. We played with my new ball, and I was captain of our side. I was elected," he said with pride.

His father smiled. "I'm glad," he said, "but I'm not too surprised. A friendly boy is bound to make friends. Now you know these boys better, and they know you better, too. You'll probably get along fairly well now."

Lennie nodded. "First, I didn't have any friends in school. Then I had Terry. He's my best friend. Now there's Jack and Joe, who like to play ball with me." Lennie smiled at his father and mother.

"I like school better every day, a *little* better, anyway," he said.

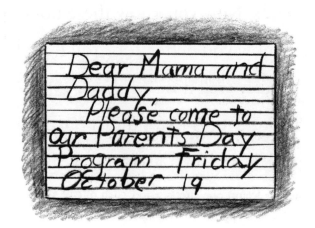

Dear Mama and Daddy,
Please come to our Parents Day Program Friday October 19

3

For some weeks everything went all right for Lennie. He liked the new school better all the time. He did make more friends. It did not seem to matter anymore that he was the only black boy in Miss Baker's room. Indeed, the color of his skin seemed of no more importance now than the color of his clothes. Lennie was happy. His parents were happy.

Then he ran into trouble again.

It was all on account of something called a "Parents' Day Program."

One morning Miss Baker had a great piece of news for her pupils.

"Our room," she said, "has been asked to give a program. It will be the first Parents' Day Program of the year."

Lennie pricked up his ears. He had never heard of a Parents' Day Program at the old school.

Miss Baker went on: "We give a Parents' Day Program every year. It's to help the parents get acquainted with one another and with our new school. We shall give a little play. The Rhythm Band will have a number. We shall learn a few songs. It will be lots of fun."

It didn't sound like fun to Lennie. He had never been in a school program. He didn't want a part in this one. He was sure that he couldn't do as well as the others. He hoped Miss Baker wouldn't ask him to play in the Rhythm Band,

or be in a play, or sing a song. He liked Miss
Baker very much, and he would like to please
her, but he didn't want any part in the program.
The very thought of it scared him till his legs
felt wobbly.

One thing he could do, and that was to write
a copy of the invitation which the teacher
put on the blackboard. This was the writing
lesson for the day. Then, of course, he must
take it home to his father and mother. It was
addressed to them.

When his father and mother read it, they
smiled at each other and at Lennie, too.

"Of course, we'll be glad to come,"
they told him.

Lennie was ashamed to tell them that he
wouldn't have a part in the program, that he
didn't want to be in the play, and that he didn't
want to help sing. He still had a scary feeling

inside himself whenever he thought about standing up with the other children.

Lennie went off in the living room. He sat by himself in a corner with a book on his lap, but he wasn't reading. He was having worry thoughts all to himself.

At supper he hardly ate a thing, though his mother had baked his favorite cake. It was chocolate with white icing at least an inch thick.

"Lennie, have you a pain in your middle?" his mother asked.

Lennie shook his head quickly. "No, ma'am!" He answered her in a hurry, because when he had a pain in his middle, his mother gave him a big dose of bitter medicine.

His father looked at him keenly. "Maybe Lennie's got the mulligrubs. That is a mighty bad thing to have. Have you got the mulligrubs, son?"

Now mulligrubs are gloomy, sad feelings, and Lennie felt bound to tell the truth.

"Yes, I guess I've got the mulligrubs," he said, but still he didn't want to talk about the reason for his gloomy, sad feelings. He was glad that his folks didn't ask him questions. He didn't want to explain.

Lennie's mother looked at him anxiously. "There's something the matter with the boy. Maybe it's not a pain in the middle, maybe it's mulligrubs, but bed's a good place for it anyway. So right to bed you're going to go, young man!"

Lennie felt sorry that he hadn't hidden his mulligrubs better. He hated to go to bed so early. It wasn't even dark yet!

After Lennie was in bed, his father brought his banjo and sat by him. He didn't ask a question. He just leaned back in his chair and began to twang the strings and hum a tune Lennie knew and liked—"The Wishing Song."

"Sing it, Daddy!" Lennie begged.

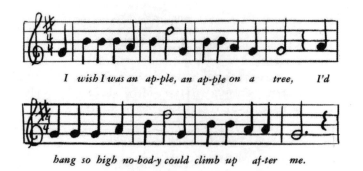

I wish I was an ap-ple, an ap-ple on a tree, I'd

bang so high no-bod-y could climb up af-ter me.

Lennie's father sang:

"I wish I was an apple,

An apple on a tree,

I'd hang so high nobody

Could climb up after me."

"Sing on, Daddy," Lennie begged.

His father went on singing. Before the song was done, Lennie was fast asleep.

"Bed's a good cure for bad feelings, mulligrubs, especially," his mother said when his father tiptoed out of Lennie's room and closed the door.

His father nodded and hung the banjo back in place on its peg.

The next morning Lennie got up feeling much better and hungrier, too. He proved it by eating three pancakes with honey before he left for school.

Once in school, though, he didn't feel so well. In fact, when they began to talk about the program, Lennie began to feel worse and worse. It was strange.

All of a sudden he said before everyone, "I don't want to be in the program!" He didn't mean to be rude or let his voice ring out so loud, but some of the children giggled.

Miss Baker said, "Very well, Lennie, we will talk about it later on."

Lennie went to the back of the room and played at the sand table. Nobody paid any attention to him. Lennie started to hum the song his father had sung to him last night.

Soon he began singing in a low tone that was almost a whisper:

"I wish I was an apple,
An apple on a tree,
I'd hang so high nobody
Could climb up after me."

Soon he was singing aloud as he made a house in the sand.

"I like that song," said Terry, coming up. "It has a pretty tune. Is that all there is to it?"

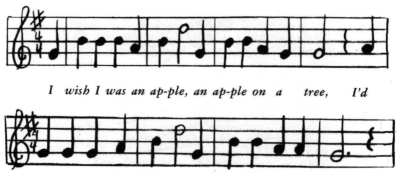

I wish I was an ap-ple, an ap-ple on a tree, I'd

hang so high no-bod-y could climb up af-ter me.

Lennie shook his head.

"You mean there is more, then? Sing the rest of it!" Terry begged. "I'd like to hear it."

Lennie glanced around. Nobody else was paying any attention to him and Terry. They were busy about their own play and talking among themselves. Lennie went on with the song.

By this time, Terry was whistling the tune.
All of a sudden, Lennie noticed that the whole
room was clapping. Then he knew that they had
overheard his song and were cheering him.

"Lennie must be in the program!" they cried.
"Lennie must sing that song."

Everyone was smiling at him, including
Miss Baker.

The friendly feeling all about him was warmer than the sunshine that filled the corner of the room. Lennie tried to smile back.

"But—but what if I get scared at the last minute when I get up before everybody, all by myself? I might forget or make a mistake," he muttered.

The very thought made him wince.

"I know how you feel," said Terry. "When
we had our first program this year, I felt a
little scared, too. You see I was a new boy, too,
when school began. It was hard for me to stand
up with the others at that time. I was afraid
I'd forget that bird call that I had to whistle.
But I didn't. I remembered all right. I bet you
will, too."

"Go ahead!" came the shout. "Go ahead,
Lennie, Terry. Do the song together. Terry can
whistle it. Lennie can sing."

Lennie found it no trouble at all to throw
back his head and open his mouth as Terry
stepped up beside him and puckered his lips to
whistle the merry tune.

After that Lennie and Terry went off to
practice. Both boys felt bound to do their best
in this very special song. That's what Miss Baker
had called it.

That night he told his parents, "I have a part on the program."

"Good for you!" his father said, looking very pleased.

"Tell us about it," his mother begged.

Lennie looked from one to the other. "If you don't mind," he told them, "I'd like to keep it for a surprise."

4

Finally, Parents' Day came. All that morning Miss Baker's room practiced the program for the afternoon. The play was rehearsed three times. The Rhythm Band wiggled and giggled as they tried over and over to keep up with the tune as Miss Baker played it on the piano.

Lennie and his partner Terry tried not to worry. They had practiced their song over and over so that they wouldn't forget a word or a note. Still, the boys couldn't help feeling just a little bit frightened for fear they might forget anyway.

Finally, the program time came. The schoolroom was crowded with fathers and mothers. Miss Baker welcomed everyone. She seemed glad to see Lennie's father and mother and gave them a front seat where they could see all that went on.

The play was given without a hitch. The Rhythm Band performed with only one or two small mistakes nobody seemed to mind.

Then Miss Baker made an announcement:

"The last number on our program is a special song by our newest pupil, Lennie Lane. It is called 'The Wishing Song,' and Terry Cole whistles the accompaniment."

Lennie found himself by Terry's side, standing up before all the people. Right there in the front row, he saw his parents. He saw the anxious look on his mother's face and the encouraging nod his father gave him. He mustn't disappoint them now. Lennie got ready to start "The Wishing Song" by drawing a great, long breath. At the same moment, Terry puckered up his lips and started to whistle the tune that rang out as sweetly as the notes of some wild bird.

"I wish I was an apple,
An apple on a tree,
I'd hang so high nobody
Could climb up after me."

"I wish I was redbird,
A redbird in a tree,
I'd fly so high nobody
Could throw a rock at me."

"I wish I was a squirrel,
A squirrel in a tree,
I'd hide so quick no hunter
Could take a shot at me."

Almost before the song was done, the people started cheering. Lennie was so excited he nearly forgot to bow, but then he remembered his manners. A good thing he did, because Terry had nearly forgotten, too! When Lennie bowed, Terry bowed. Then they both bowed together.

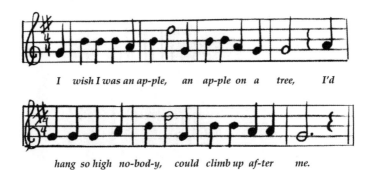

I wish I was an ap-ple,   an ap-ple on a   tree,   I'd

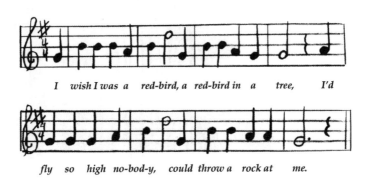

hang so high no-bod-y,   could climb up af-ter   me.

I wish I was a   red-bird, a red-bird in a   tree,   I'd

fly   so   high no-bod-y,   could throw a   rock at   me.

I wish I was a   squir-rel, a squir-rel in a   tree,   I'd

hide so quick no   hun-ter could take a shot at   me.

The applause followed them back to their seat.

"Just listen, will you?" whispered Terry. "They are cheering louder and longer for us than for anyone else."

Lennie nodded. "And I know why. I can tell you the reason for all that cheering. You remember the teacher said ours was a very special song."

"That's important, I guess," Terry whispered.

But Lennie hardly heard what Terry said. He was looking at his father and mother—the happy smile on his mother's lips, the proud look on his father's face. He knew they were glad because he wasn't any longer a new boy in school. Now he belonged to the school just like everybody else.